Rebecca Hobbs' stories are inspired by her day-to-day experiences in the classroom as a primary school teacher and being with her own two young children. When not covered in paint, head to toe in glitter or 'eating' playdough creations, Rebecca enjoys writing stories for children, combining relatable themes with a little touch of magic. She is a fan of biscuits, cardigans and daydreaming.

To Emily,
Quick! Catch it!
Love Rebecca

Rebecca Hobbs
CAUGHT IT

AUSTIN MACAULEY PUBLISHERS™
LONDON • CAMBRIDGE • NEW YORK • SHARJAH

A CIP catalogue record for this title is available from the British Library.

ISBN 9781528950213 (Paperback)
ISBN 9781528972604 (ePub e-book)

www.austinmacauley.com

First Published (2021)
Austin Macauley Publishers Ltd
25 Canada Square
Canary Wharf
London
E14 5LQ

For Fred and Evie.

It was Evie's first day at school and she was excitedly skipping across the playground towards her new teacher, Miss Fletcher.

Welcome to school!

She stopped and turned to give a final wave goodbye to her mum, who smiled, waved back and blew Evie a kiss.

Suddenly, Evie felt very sad and tears filled her big brown eyes. She knew she would miss her mum so much today.

"Catch it!" Miss Fletcher whispered in Evie's ear.
Evie shot out her open hand and quickly closed it, catching the kiss so it couldn't escape.

"Caauuught it?" Evie said, puzzled, looking at her closed fist.
"Catch all the kisses that come your way. They'll make you feel loved all through the day,"
Miss Fletcher simply explained.

Evie smiled, feeling delighted and quickly put her mum's precious kiss in her coat pocket.

She continued to skip happily into the classroom knowing she'd have a little bit of Mummy with her all day.
Miss Fletcher was showing them all where to hang up their coats and bags.
Evie's peg was next to her best friend Amelia's peg.

She gently placed her hand in her coat pocket and scooped up Mummy's kiss, carefully putting it in her cardigan pocket.

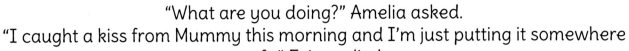

"What are you doing?" Amelia asked.
"I caught a kiss from Mummy this morning and I'm just putting it somewhere safe," Evie replied.
"Why?" Amelia giggled.

HELEN HENRY ANNA FRANK ELINA MAY FR

16

"Catch all the kisses that come your way. They'll make you feel loved all through the day," Evie whispered and blew Amelia a kiss.
"Caught it!" Amelia squealed and blew one right back to Evie.
"Caught it!" Evie sang and placed it gently in her pocket next to Mummy's kiss.
Miss Fletcher smiled as she heard this and quickly tapped her pocket that held the kiss she had caught from her little boy that morning.

Evie was having the best morning. She had played in the sand tray, painted, counted to ten and sang her most favourite nursery rhymes.

18

But now they had stopped to get ready
for lunch and Evie was missing
her mummy.

"Catch all the kisses that come your way.
They'll make you feel loved all through
the day."

Evie suddenly remembered her treasured
kiss and put her hand in her pocket. She was
immediately enveloped
in a warm, invisible hug and felt better.

With the kiss safe in her pocket she followed her class as they made their way to lunch.
Following lunch, out in the playground, Evie spotted her big brother, Fred. He had just fallen over whilst playing football and was clutching his leg.

Fred looked upset but as soon as he saw Evie, he managed a weak smile and waved.
Evie tapped her pocket, smiled and blew Fred a kiss.

"Catch all the kisses that come your way. They'll make you feel loved all through the day," she called to him.

Fred raised his hand, "Caught it!" he shouted, laughing, thinking how funny his little sister was but strangely forgetting about his sore leg, running off to re-join the game.

Wow! Catching kisses really is magical! Evie happily thought to herself and went to find Amelia.

The rest of the day flew by and anytime Evie missed Mummy she put her hand in the her pocket and thought of her special caught kiss.

24

After school, Evie went to Grandma's house for tea. They chatted excitedly about Evie's first day, danced, sang and ate cake, lots of cake.

It was always so much fun being with Grandma and time always went by so quickly. In a flash, it was time for Evie to go and Grandma suddenly looked a little sad.
Evie knew just what to do and as she was getting into her daddy's car; she blew Grandma a kiss.

"Catch all the kisses that come your way. They'll make you feel loved all through the day."

"Caught it!" Grandma chuckled and blew one right back to Evie, who quickly placed it with her other kisses.

As soon as Evie got home she ran through the front door, shouting, "Mummy! Mummy! I caught it!"

"Caught it?!" Mummy asked confused.

"Yes, Mummy! I caught your kiss! Didn't you know...?

"Catch all the kisses that come your way. They'll make you feel loved all through the day."

Evie then blew her mummy a kiss and as she ran up the stairs she heard her mummy happily call out,

"CAUGHT IT!"